For Rachael
– Adam

For my mom and dad
– Nina

Copyright © 2021 Clavis Publishing Inc., New York

Visit us on the Web at www.clavis-publishing.com.

Maybe I'll Be written by Adam Ciccio and illustrated by Nina Podlesnyak

ISBN 978-1-60537-651-6

This book was printed in August 2021 at Nikara, M. R. Štefánika 858/25, 963 01 Krupina, Slovakia.

First Edition
10 9 8 7 6 5 4 3 2 1

Maybe I'll Be

Written by Adam Ciccio
Illustrated by Nina Podlesnyak

Clavis

NEW YORK

My sister wants to be an *astronaut!* How does she know?
She's so sure of her dreams, and just waiting to grow.

What do I want to be? I need to know *more*.

I hope it's okay to wait, to wonder, *to explore.*

Maybe I'll be *a doctor* and help people that are sick.

Maybe I'll be *a magician.*
Want to see a cool magic trick?

Maybe I'll be *a boat-builder* and sail the ocean all summer.

Maybe I'll be *a mechanic,*
            a welder,
                  or *a plumber.*

Maybe I'll be *a judge* and choose right from wrong.

Maybe I'll be *a performer.* Want to hear me sing a song?

Maybe I'll be *a pilot* and take my wings to the sky!
I won't choose now and let my dream pass me by.

Maybe I'll *drive fast cars* . . .

. . . but figuring it out isn't a race.

I'll be happy for my sister,
who will one day shoot into space.

I'll be here on Earth, just dreaming away.
I'll be satisfied just being me . . .
yesterday, tomorrow, and today.